THIS BAD MOOD
BELONGS TO:

First published in Great Britain in 2017 by Andersen Press Ltd.,
20 Vauxhall Bridge Road, London SW1V 2SA
Originally published in the USA by Little, Brown and Company,
Hachette Book Group, 1290 Avenue of the Americas, New York, NY 10104

Printed and bound in China.

First Edition
ISBN 978 1 78344 642 1

British Library Cataloguing in Publication Data available.

The Bad Mood and the Stick

Lemony Snicket

Art by Matthew Forsythe

Andersen Press

Once there was a stick and a bad mood.

The stick was on the ground,

and the bad mood was with a girl named Curly.

Curly had been with the bad mood for two hours, since she had seen an ice cream shop but hadn't got any ice cream.

The stick had been on the ground since
last night, when the tree dropped it.

Curly picked up the stick and used it to poke her brother.

"That's not nice," said her mother. "Apologise to Napoleon and throw the stick in the bushes."

Curly had really enjoyed poking her brother Napoleon –
so much that her bad mood was gone.

Her mother was carrying it now. "Harrumph," she said, which
is a bad mood noise.

The stick didn't say anything,

even when a raccoon picked it up.

Who knows what the raccoon wanted to do with the stick,

but he ran out of the bushes
and frightened an old man
named Lou.

"Holy moly!" said Lou, which is what he
always said when something exciting
happened, and his feet did a little danc

and he fell into a puddle.

Curly's mother couldn't help herself and started to laugh.

Her bad mood was gone.

Lou had it.

The sound of all that laughter startled the raccoon, and he dropped the stick in the mud.

"Look at my dungarees," Lou said, which was *his* bad mood noise. "They're a muddy awful mess."

The stick didn't answer.

Lou went straight to the dry cleaner's. A lady named Mrs Durham was head of the establishment, with a pencil behind her ear.

"Take that pencil outta your ear," said Lou. "You gotta wash these dungarees and wash them quick. I'll stand around here in my underwear until you're done."

"You will do no such thing," said Mrs Durham. "This is a family place."

But Lou already had his dungarees off. "Here you go," he said. "They're a muddy awful mess."

"Ugh," said Mrs Durham, looking at the dungarees and looking at Lou, and you would think that the bad mood would have moved on to her.

But it didn't.

She took one look at Lou in his underwear,
and the bad mood flew right out of the window.

You never know what is going to happen.

Same thing with the stick. You would never guess, but some kind of bug made a brightly coloured cocoon on it.

"Well, look at that," said Bert, and picked it up to look at it better.

He took it back to his ice cream shop and put it on display.

"That's unusual," said Curly's mother, when they walked by.
"What do you say, kids? Let's all have some ice cream."

Curly had fudge ripple and Napoleon had mint choc chip.
Curly's mother ordered vanilla yogurt, but then she changed
her mind and had fudge ripple, too.

This didn't bother Bert. The bad mood was nowhere around.

By the time Lou arrived, with his dungarees all clean and pressed, he wanted a double scoop, and so did Mrs Durham.

"Holy moly," Lou said, "do I love ice cream."

Mrs Durham smiled. "Same here," she said.

And three years later they were married. The wedding was
right there in the park and everyone in this book was invited.

Even the raccoon. Curly and Napoleon carried the flowers and they did a great job. You never know what is going to happen.

By then the bad mood had been all around the world.

You yourself had it several times.

The stick, however, stayed in the ice cream shop.
The cocoon had opened a long time ago,
and Bert had helped the bug fly out into the world,

but the stick he kept right there. It put him in a good mood.